How My Library Grew
by Dinah

ABOUT THE AUTHOR

MARTHA ALEXANDER is the author and illustrator of many well loved children's books. Born in Augusta, Georgia, she studied at the Cincinnati Academy of Arts, taught art in Honolulu, and later became a magazine and fashion illustrator in New York City.

In 1965 she began illustrating children's books and shortly thereafter tried her hand at illustrating her own stories. The first of these was *Out! Out! Out!* (1968). *Blackboard Bear*, published in 1969, was included in *The New York Times* Outstanding Books of 1969. The next year *Bobo's Dream* was voted one of the Best Books of the Year by *School Library Journal*.

Since that time Martha Alexander has created many popular books, including three more *Blackboard Bear* books and *Nobody Asked Me If I Wanted a Baby Sister*; *I'll Protect You from the Jungle Beasts*; *Marty McGee's Space Lab*, *No Girls Allowed* and *Move Over, Twerp*.

Speaking of how she comes up with the ideas for her books Martha Alexander says, "My subject matter comes from my grandchildren and from other children. I also use the feelings I remember from my own childhood."

How My Library Grew
by Dinah

Story and Pictures by Martha Alexander

THE H. W. WILSON COMPANY • NEW YORK

Happy ninetieth birthday
to a wonderful lady, my aunt,
Fannie Lu

Library of Congress Cataloging in Publication Data

Alexander, Martha G.
    How my library grew, by Dinah.

Summary: Neither Dinah nor her Teddy Bear have ever
been to a library, but when one is built just down the
street, she looks forward to the opening day.
    [1. Libraries—Fiction]   I. Title.
PZ7.A3777Ho   1983   [E]   82-20204
ISBN 0-8242-0670-3

```
jE A
Alexander, Martha G.
How my library grew, by
 Dinah :
```

Manufactured in the United States of America.

I wonder what all that noise is?
Teddy, look! There's a bulldozer across the street
and it's digging a big hole.

What's happening across the street, Mommy?
Well, Dinah, we're going to have a new library.
All that machinery will help build it.

A library? What's that?
A library is a building where books are kept
for people to borrow.
For me and Teddy too?
Sure, for you and Teddy too.

We better get dressed so we can go watch
them build our library.

Look at all that dirt they're taking out of there, Teddy.

Now they're hauling it away.

That hole is getting bigger and bigger.

I wonder if the library will fit in it now.

Hi, Dad. Are you going to help them build the library?
No, Dinah. I'm going to plant our vegetable garden.

Oh, no! There's a pesky mole here. See that mole hill?
What do moles eat, Daddy?
I'm not sure, but I hope it's not vegetables.

How many more days until the library's finished?
Oh, Dinah, it will take a long, long time.
All summer and fall, maybe until after Christmas.

How are we ever going to wait, Teddy?
We'd better fix a place to watch from.
My old high chair would be perfect.

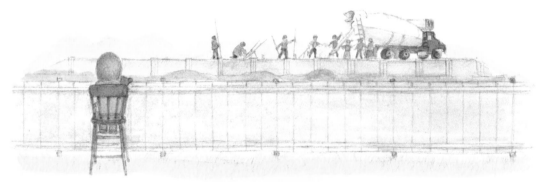

Look, that's a cement mixer.
That soupy stuff they're pouring is cement.
It will get hard like stone after a while.
Daddy told me about it.

I think the foundation is finished now.
That's to hold the building up.

See, that's where the walls are going to be.
Those poles are sort of like the skeleton.

Oh, no! It's raining and they're not building today.
At least the rain will make the garden grow, Dinah.
But I want it to stop so the library can grow.
I feel like it will *never* get finished.

Mommie, look! A rainbow! What makes rainbows, Mommie?
Water drops, I think.
But how?
I really don't know, Dinah.

It's cold out, Teddy.
I'll put your sweater on.

Now they're building
the roof.

Hello, Mister.
Is the library finished yet?

No, not yet. The outside is almost
finished, but not the inside.

Just be patient, Teddy.
They *have* finished the outside.

I can't see what
they're doing anymore.

It's snowing so hard I can
hardly even see the library.

Good news, Dinah!
Our library will open next month.
A month! That's a long time.

What's the matter? You look miserable.
I've been making a surprise for the library.
It's a secret. But now I can't finish it.

Why not?
Because I need to see how they build the *inside*.
Don't worry, Dinah. We'll go see the foreman soon.

The electrician puts in wiring,
and the plumber puts in pipes.

This plasterboard is for the walls.
Pretty soon the painters will come.

Finally, the bookshelves will be built.
Then your library will be finished.

Tomorrow is opening day.
Our surprise is almost ready.

Everyone is coming. I see Patrick and his brother,
and Harriet, and Stevie and his whole family.
I hope there will be enough books left for me and Teddy.

This present is for the library.
It's a book called "How my Library Grew."
I made the pictures and Mommy wrote the words for me.
That's wonderful, Dinah.
We'll put your book on the bulletin board for everyone to see.

Hi, Bruce. What are you doing in the children's room?
Hi, Dinah. I'm the children's librarian.
I didn't know that.
Do you have any books about moles and rainbows?

I'm sure we do. Let's see what we can find.
But, Bruce, this mole is wearing clothes.
Moles don't wear clothes, do they?
And rainbows don't have wings either.

Nature Corner

I guess you want information about *real* moles and *real* rainbows. We'll look right here in the Nature section.

Check Out

You can sit here and look through all these books.
Then you can choose the ones you want to borrow.

How many can I borrow, Bruce?
As many as you like. We'll put them on your mother's card.
But why can't I have my own?
When you're a little older and can write your name,
you can have your own card.

Look what I got at the library! A book that tells what
moles eat and one about how rainbows are made.
Now we can find out all about them.

Please, Daddy, would you show me how to write my name?
I want to learn to write it myself.
I want my *own* library card.

Look, Daddy, look, Daddy, look!
I did it! I practiced all day and now I can write my name.

Come on, Dinah. We'll go get your card.

I can write my name now, Bruce. I came to get my library card.

Well, Dinah, I'm delighted.
I think you'll be our youngest card owner!

Mommie, Mommie, I got my card! Here are some books
I can read to myself and to Teddy.
They have only pictures, no words.
And I brought a book for you too. On *my* card.

Listen carefully, Teddy. I'm going to read you a bedtime story. It's a special book about a Teddy Bear. And guess what? His name is Teddy too.